The Heron and the Fish

RETOLD AND ILLUSTRATED BY GRAHAM PERCY

For Taio and Eva

Distributed in the United States of America by
The Child's World®
1980 Lookout Drive • Mankato, MN 56003-1705
800-599-READ • www.childsworld.com

ACKNOWLEDGMENTS
The Child's World®: Mary Berendes, Publishing Director
The Design Lab: Kathleen Petelinsek, Art Direction and Design;
Anna Petelinsek, Page Production

LIBRARY OF CONGRESS CATALOGING-IN-PUBLICATION DATA
Percy, Graham.
 The heron and the fish / retold and illustrated by Graham Percy.
    p. cm. — (Aesop's fables)
 Summary: A hungry heron learns a lesson about being too choosy when he
spends all day looking for the perfect meal.
 ISBN 978-1-60253-202-1 (lib. bound : alk. paper)
 [1. Fables. 2. Folklore.] I. Aesop. II. Title.
 PZ8.2.P435He 2009
 398.2—dc22
 [E]   2009001587

MORAL

Being too picky might leave you with nothing at all.

One sunny afternoon, a proud heron was strolling along a sparkling stream. He had spent the morning looking at his reflection. He thought he was a very beautiful bird.

Now he was beginning to feel hungry. What could such a special bird as he have for supper?

Just ahead of him, two fat perch were playing. They were so busy with their game, they didn't notice the heron approaching.

The heron could have easily gobbled them both up. Instead, he walked past them with his beak in the air.

"Far too boring and tasteless for me," said the heron. "I can't be bothered even to open my beak for them."

Further along the stream, two large trout were splashing about. The water churned and foamed as the fish chased each other in circles.

The heron shook his head as he passed them.

"Far too much trouble to catch," he complained. "I'm sure to find something much better around the next bend."

He strolled on.

A school of tiny minnows darted past his feet. The heron looked down at the fish in disgust.

"Far too small and bony," he said. "A heron of my size needs much bigger fish than that."

The heron strutted on. It wasn't long before he saw a fat carp resting in a shady pool.

"Far too scaly for me," complained the heron. He kept strolling. "Will I find nothing to eat today?" he grumbled.

By now, the heron was very, very hungry. The sun was going down, and it would soon be dark. Then the heron would not be able to see anything in the water.

The heron began to worry. He swished his beak this way and that. He searched among the pebbles and weeds looking for something—anything—to eat.

At last, he found a tiny snail. With a swoosh of his beak, he scooped it up and gulped it down his throat.

All the fish gathered to watch the heron. They giggled and gurgled at his small and tasteless supper.

A wise old toad had been watching the heron all day. He rubbed his chin and said loudly, "Being too picky might leave you with nothing at all."

AESOP

Aesop was a storyteller who lived more than 2,500 years ago. He lived so long ago, there isn't much information about him. Most people believe Aesop was a slave who lived in the area around the Mediterranean Sea—probably in or near the country of Greece.

Aesop's fables are known in almost every culture in the world, in almost every language. His fables are even *part* of some languages! Some common phrases come from Aesop's fables, such as "sour grapes" and "Don't count your chickens before they're hatched."

ABOUT FABLES

Fables are one of the oldest forms of stories. They are often short and funny, and have animals as the main characters. These animals act like people. Often, fables teach the reader a lesson. This is called a *moral*. A moral might teach right from wrong, or show how to act in good, kind ways. A moral might show what happens when someone makes a poor decision. Fables teach us how to live wisely.

ABOUT THE ILLUSTRATOR

Graham Percy was a famous illustrator of more than one hundred books. He was born and raised in New Zealand. He first studied art at the Elam School of Art in New Zealand and then moved to London, England, to study at the Royal College of Art.

Mr. Percy especially loved to draw animals, many types of which can be found in his books. He illustrated books on everything from mysteries to lullabies. He was even a designer for the animated film "Hugo the Hippo." Mr. Percy lived most of his life in London.